*For David and Amelia*
M.W.

*For Charlie*
B.F.

First published 1991 by
Walker Books Ltd, 87 Vauxhall Walk
London SE11 5HJ

Text © 1991 Martin Waddell
Illustrations © 1991 Barbara Firth

First printed 1991
Printed and bound in Hong Kong by
South China Printing Co. (1988) Ltd

British Library Cataloguing in Publication Data
Waddell, Martin *1941-*
Let's go home, Little Bear.
I. Title II. Firth, Barbara
823.914 [J]

ISBN 0-7445-1912-8

# LET'S GO HOME, LITTLE BEAR

Written by
**Martin Waddell**

Illustrated by
**Barbara Firth**

WALKER BOOKS
LONDON

Once there were two bears.

Big Bear and Little Bear.

Big Bear is the big bear

and Little Bear is the little bear.

They went for a walk in the woods.

They walked and they walked and
they walked until Big Bear said,
"Let's go home, Little Bear."
So they started back home on the
path through the woods.

PLOD PLOD PLOD

went Big Bear, plodding along.

Little Bear ran on in front,

jumping and sliding

and having great fun.

And then . . .

Little Bear stopped

and he listened

and then he turned round

and he looked.

"Come on, Little Bear," said Big Bear,

 but Little Bear didn't stir.

"I thought I heard something!" Little Bear said.

"What did you hear?" said Big Bear.

"Plod, plod, plod," said Little Bear.

"I think it's a Plodder!"

 Big Bear turned round and

 he listened and looked.

 No Plodder was there.

"Let's go home, Little Bear," said Big Bear.

"The plod was my feet in the snow."

They set off again on the path

through the woods.

PLOD PLOD PLOD

went Big Bear with Little Bear

walking beside him,

just glancing a bit, now and again.

And then . . .

Little Bear stopped

and he listened

and then he turned round

and he looked.

"Come on, Little Bear," said Big Bear,

 but Little Bear didn't stir.

"I thought I heard something!"

 Little Bear said.

"What did you hear?" said Big Bear.

"Drip, drip, drip," said Little Bear.

"I think it's a Dripper!"

Big Bear turned round, and

he listened and looked.

No Dripper was there.

"Let's go home, Little Bear,"

said Big Bear.

"That was the ice as it

dripped in the stream."

They set off again on the
path through the woods.
PLOD PLOD PLOD
went Big Bear with Little Bear
closer beside him.

And then . . .
Little Bear stopped
and he listened
and then he turned round
and he looked.

"Come on, Little Bear," said Big Bear,

but Little Bear didn't stir.

"I know I heard something this time!"

Little Bear said.

"What did you hear?" said Big Bear.

"Plop, plop, plop," said Little Bear.

"I think it's a Plopper."

Big Bear turned round,

and he listened and looked.

No Plopper was there.

"Let's go home, Little Bear,"

said Big Bear.

"That was the snow plopping

down from a branch."

PLOD PLOD PLOD

went Big Bear along the path

through the woods.

But Little Bear walked

slower and slower

and at last he sat

down in the snow.

"Come on, Little Bear," said Big Bear.

"It is time we were both back home."

But Little Bear sat and said nothing.

"Come on and be carried,"

said Big Bear.

Big Bear put Little Bear

high up on his back,

and set off down the path

through the woods.

WOO WOO WOO

"It is only the wind, Little Bear,"

said Big Bear and he walked

on down the path.

CREAK CREAK CREAK

"It is only the trees, Little Bear,"

said Big Bear and he walked

on down the path.

PLOD PLOD PLOD

"It is only the sound of my feet again,"

said Big Bear, and he plodded on

and on and on until they came

back home to their cave.

Big Bear and Little Bear

went down into the dark,

the dark of their own

Bear Cave.

"Just stay there, Little Bear,"

said Big Bear, putting Little Bear

in the Bear Chair with a blanket

to keep him warm.

Big Bear stirred up the fire

from the embers

and lighted the lamps

and made the Bear Cave

all cosy again.

"Now tell me a story,"

Little Bear said.

And Big Bear sat down in the Bear Chair

with Little Bear curled on his lap.

And he told a story of Plodders

and Drippers and Ploppers

and the sounds of the snow

in the woods,

and this Little Bear

and this Big Bear

plodding all the way . . .

HOME